I0824570

Major League SOCCER

Philadelphia Union

Marty Gitlin

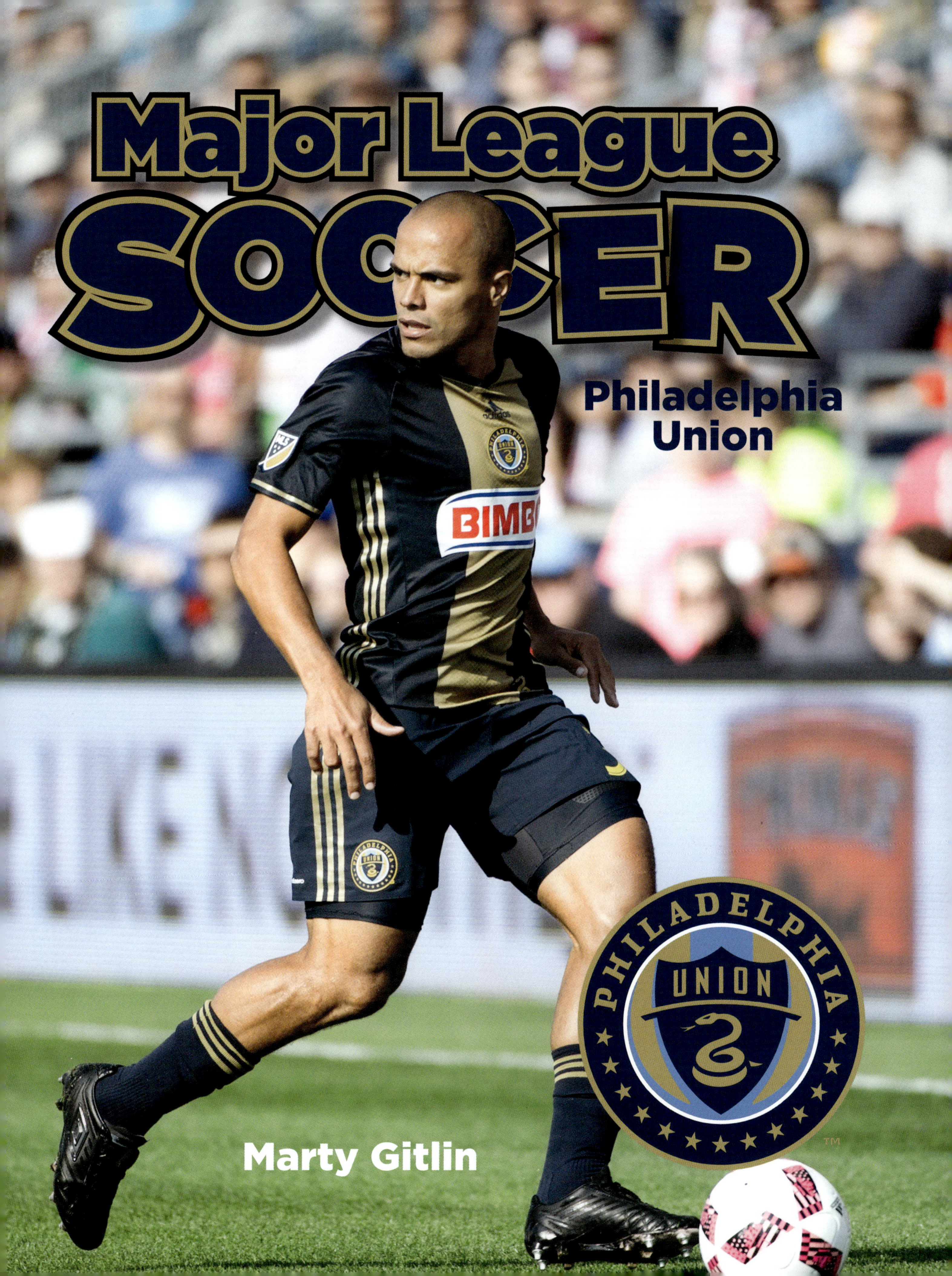

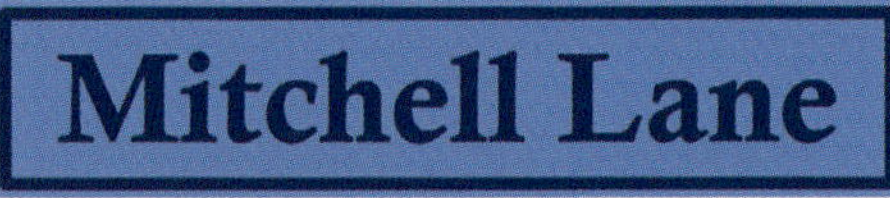

Printing 1 2 3 4 5 6 7 8

First Edition, 2020.
Author: Marty Gitlin
Designer: Ed Morgan
Editor: Lisa Petrillo

Series: Major League Soccer
Title: Philadelphia Union / by Marty Gitlin

Hallandale, FL : Mitchell Lane Publishers, [2020]

Library bound ISBN: 9781680204841
eBook ISBN: 9781680204858

PHOTO CREDITS: Design Elements, freepik.com, APImages.com, p.12-13 Something Original CC-BY-SA-3.0,

Contents

Words in **bold** throughout can be found in the Glossary.

All About MLS

Many Americans love sports. Their favorites are football, baseball, and basketball. But another game has gained popularity in recent decades. And that is soccer.

FIFA stands for the Federation Internationale de Football Association, which is French for the **International** Federation of Association Football. The organization runs the sport worldwide. It required that a professional soccer league be launched in the United States to earn the right to host the World Cup.

That demand gave birth to Major League Soccer (MLS). It began with 10 **franchises** in 1996. Officials took a modest approach to starting the venture. Some major cities did not boast a team. Even the huge city of Chicago had none.

Philadelphia Union fans cheer their team on.

An impressive average of 17,406 fans attended MLS games in its first season. The number continued to rise. It grew every year from 2013 to 2016, and peaked at 22,113 in 2017. The most successful franchise proved to be the Seattle Sounders. The Sounders averaged more than 40,000 fans per home game during that period. The Atlanta Football Club also began with a bang. It averaged a League-best 48,200 fans in its **inaugural** season of 2017.

The League continued to expand. It reached 23 teams in 2018. All but three reside in the United States. The Canadian cities of Montreal, Toronto, and Vancouver also boast franchises. The League was divided into an Eastern Conference and Western Conference from the start. There were 11 teams in the East and 12 in the West in 2018.

Chapter One

One of many positive aspects of Major League Soccer is its **diversity**. More than 60 percent of its players were born outside the United States in 2018. The number of foreign-born players has grown significantly. In 2012, more than half were Americans. California boasts the most U.S.-born MLS players by far, with 71. New York is second with 21 and Texas third with 18. Each MLS team plays 34 matches, including 17 at home and 17 on the road. Teams receive three points for every victory and one for a tie. They all battle to earn a **playoff** spot by placing among the top six in their conference. The two teams that tally the most points in each conference get to bypass the first round of the playoffs. That allows them to advance to the second round while the other teams must win a match to remain alive.

The next two rounds are two-match playoffs. The teams that score the most goals in those matches compete for the **MLS Cup** title in December. That ends a long season that begins in March. But the wait and work are worth it, especially for the team that earns the crown. One team that is still seeking its first championship is the Philadelphia Union.

Fun Facts

1. The Toronto Football Club became the first Canadian team to win the MLS Cup in 2017. Toronto shut out the defending champion Seattle Sounders to snag the title.

2. The MLS will expand again in the year 2020. There will be a total of 26 teams with the addition of franchises in Cincinnati, Nashville, and Miami. That is nearly triple the number that launched the MLS in 1996.

The Philadephia Union Story

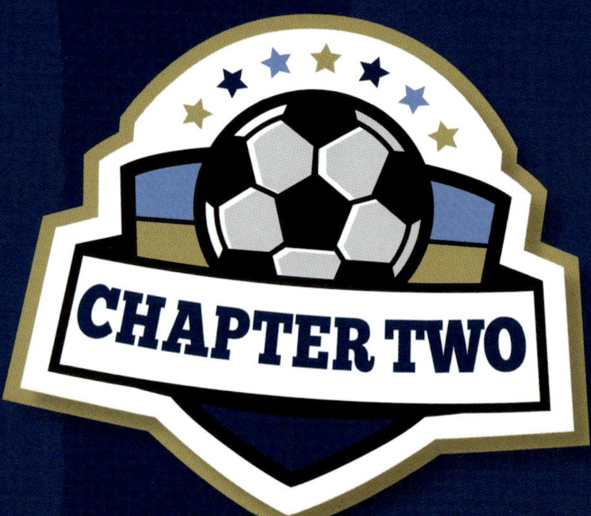

Major League Soccer had existed for 12 years when Philadelphia landed a franchise in 2008. It was awarded to the local **ownership** group of Keystone Sports and Entertainment, LLC. The team was named Philadelphia Union by a vote of fans in 2009. The team was considered so important that the mayor first announced the official name at a ceremony in the historic city.

The "Union" name honors the major role of Philadelphia in the founding of the United States. It is no wonder that the team colors are navy blue and gold. Those are the same colors worn by colonial soldiers who fought and defeated the British during the Revolutionary War to win independence.

The **crest** that represents the franchise features 13 gold stars. Each star signifies one of the original American colonies, which includes Pennsylvania. The rattlesnake shown on the shield honors a political cartoon drawn by Benjamin Franklin, a founder of our nation who was also a printer and writer, that appeared in a Philadelphia newspaper more than 200 years ago.

The Union team members played their first match on March 25, 2010. They lost to the Sounders, 2-0. But it did not take them long to earn their first victory. A 3-2 defeat of D.C. United three weeks later marked their first home match before 34,870 fans.

Philadelphia Union's Danny Mwanga (*left*) plays against Seattle Sounders' Osvaldo Alsonso in March, 2010.

That win did not launch an era of greatness for Philadelphia. The team qualified for the MLS playoffs only twice in its first eight seasons.

The Union players reached the conference **semifinals** in 2011, when they managed their only winning record. They finished third in the Eastern Conference that year with a fine 11-8-15 record while scoring 44 goals and allowing just 36. They began with a bang, winning four of their first six matches with just one defeat. They lost to the Houston Dynamo in the first round of the playoffs, scoring just one goal in two matches.

That proved to be their best season. The Union placed sixth in 2016 and lost in the final round, called a knockout round.

The team has gained greater success in U.S. Open Cup play than MLS competition. It beat the Dallas Football Club in the semifinals in 2014 before losing the championship match to Seattle. The Union players again reached the Open Cup championship round in 2015. They defeated Chicago to earn a title match against Kansas City. That battle was tied at 1-1 when the Union lost on penalty kicks. Philadelphia also qualified for the Open Cup finals in 2018.

Andre Blake of the Philadelphia Union makes a diving save in the first half of the 2015 U.S. Open Cup Final against Sporting Kansas City in September 2015.

Chapter Two

The Union has struggled greatly in MLS competition on the road, where the team has never compiled a winning record. The team has averaged just three victories a year away from home. Those problems were magnified in 2017. That year Philadelphia managed a 10-4 mark with three ties at home and won just one away match.

The losing records have hurt season fan attendance, which has dropped nearly every year. It peaked at an average of 19.254 per game in 2010, and fell to 16.812 in 2017.

The Union plays home matches at Talen Energy Stadium in the suburb of Chester, five miles south of Philadelphia. The venue opened its doors June 27, 2010. It holds up to 18,500 fans and boasts a natural grass field.

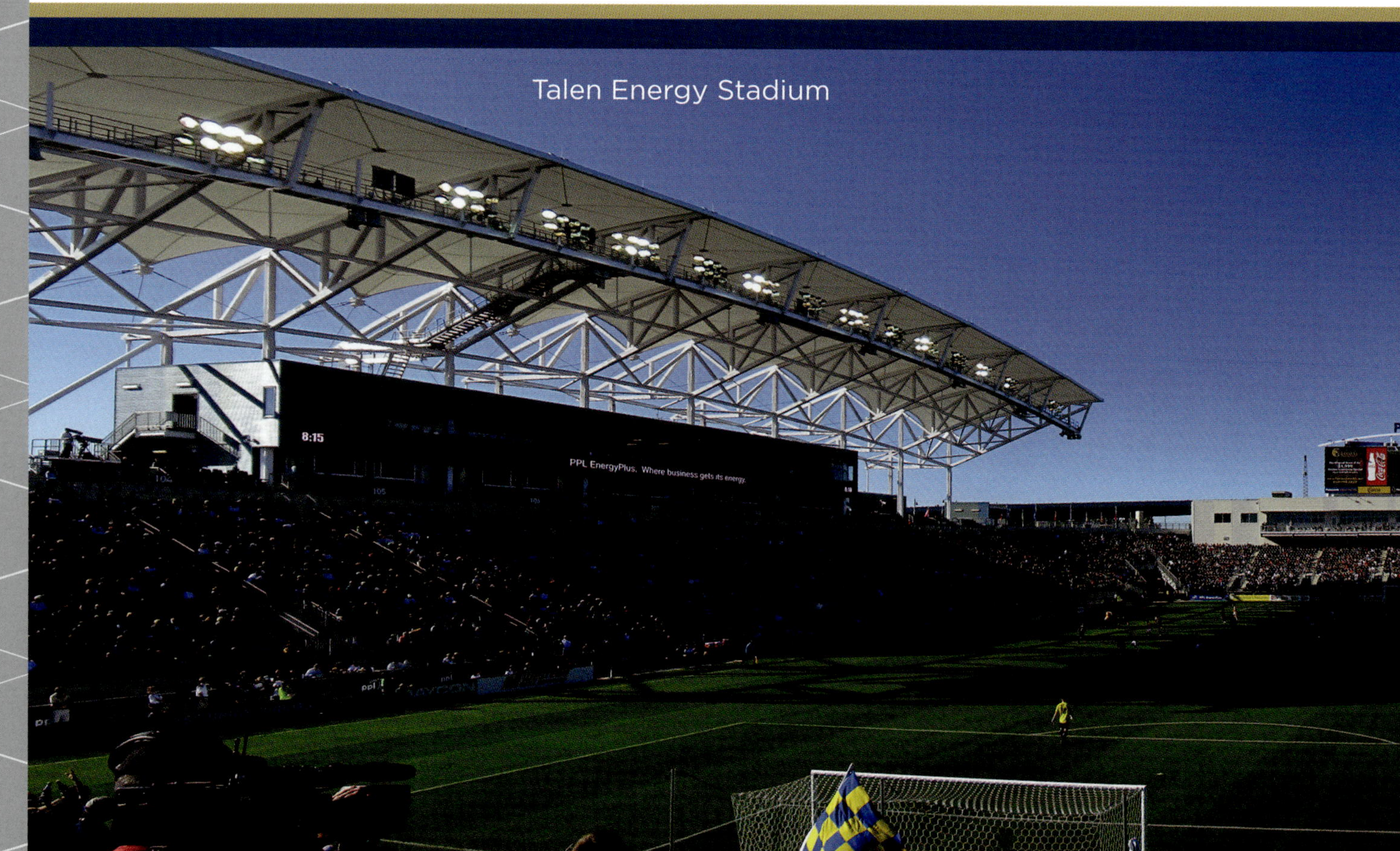

Talen Energy Stadium

Fun Facts

1 The Union has finished a season with more wins than losses just once in eight years. The team managed a record of 11-8-15 in 2011. The 15 ties remain a franchise record. Its overall record from 2010 to 2017 stood at 83-110-75.

2 Philadelphia has finished under .500 at home just once. The 2012 Union finished with a 7-8-2 mark in home games. But the team has never won more than five games on the road in any season.

Playing Our Game

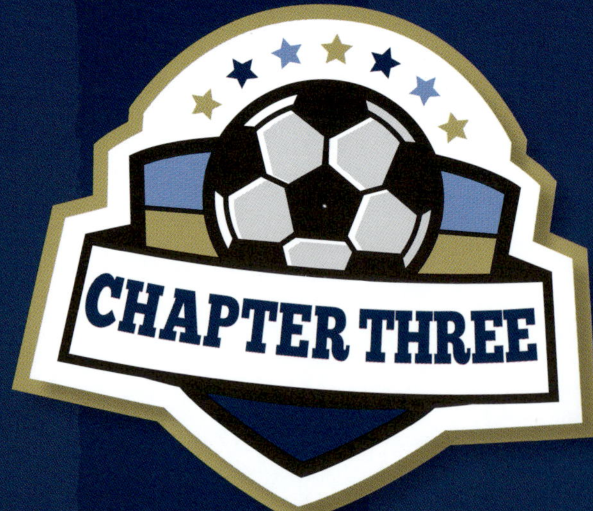

Imagine you are playing in a Major League Soccer match in the forward position. The score is 0-0, and time is running out. The ball is passed to you. The only player standing in the way of you and the net is the goalkeeper. You know that one goal will mean victory. After all, many MLS matches end in a 1-0 score. Your shot must be perfect.

You have received help from your teammates. One of the defenders stole the ball from an opponent. He passed it to a wing, who delivered it right to your feet. You are racing ahead as you move the ball from one foot to the other. You then boot it with every bit of power you can muster. The ball flies toward the right corner of the goal. The goalkeeper dives, but it is just out of his reach. The ball slams into the net.

Goalkeeper(GK)
Right back defender (RB)
Left back defender (LB)
Center back defender (CB)
Left midfielder (LM)
Center midfielder (CM)
Right midfielder (RM)
Left forward (LF)
Right forward (RF)

Your team wins 1-0. But you know you did not win it by yourself. All your teammates helped. That is how champions play. Everyone chips in.

Among your teammates are the defenders. Their task is to prevent shots on goal. They try to steal the ball or kick it away from opponents. The first line of defense comes from three midfielders and two wingbacks. The midfielders are fittingly named because they roam around midfield. So do the wingbacks. But they play near the sidelines.

Four other defenders are positioned between them and the goalkeeper. They are the fullbacks and center-backs. The two fullbacks work near the sidelines. The center-backs defend the middle of the field.

The last line of defense is the goalkeeper. His job is to prevent booted balls from landing in the net. He must react and move his feet fast. He must also leap and stretch in any direction quickly to stop shots kicked at great speeds from close range.

Chapter Three

Everyone else on the field has at least some responsibility to help the offense. Included are the two center midfielders. The attacking midfielders try to control and pass the ball to set up scores.

Wings and forwards work closest to the net. They are counted on to score. They sometimes even bounce the ball off their heads past goalkeepers. Such shots are called headers. Forwards generally score more goals than any other players. That places the spotlight on them. But every player on the field is critical to the success of a team.

The teams with the top talent earn titles. Those that win the most matches create the best **rivalries**. MLS features many heated rivalries. Some are based on great playoff matches in the past. Other teams become rivals with opponents located in nearby cities.

Philadelphia Union forward Cory Burke (*left*) beats New England Revolution defender Antonio Mlinar Delamea in August 2018.

That is the case with the Philadelphia Union. Philly's biggest rival is D.C. United, whose home is just 140 miles away. The Union has also established a rivalry with the New York Red Bulls. Philadelphia has not enjoyed enough success on the field to maintain a rivalry against any foe based on playoff competition.

The team's road woes have also hurt. But it is hard for MLS teams to win away from home. Long plane travel and living out of hotels can sap energy. And cheering fans help players perform better. Home teams often beat foes with greater talent.

The Union most often has not been the team with better talent. Such was not the case in 2011. That is when they were among the top defensive clubs in Major League Soccer. Philly surrendered just 36 goals in 34 games that year. Only the Los Angeles Galaxy allowed fewer.

Philadelphia has never won a playoff game. But it has boasted many great players during its short time in Major League Soccer.

Fun Facts

1 The Union has struggled to win matches over the years. But not against its biggest **rival**. Philly owns an 11-8-4 record against D.C. United. That includes an 8-3 mark at home.

2 Many U.S. sports fans complain about a lack of offense in soccer. Teams rarely score more than three goals. The only exception in an MLS Cup final was in 2003. That is when San Jose scored four to defeat Chicago.

Best of the Union

The player that scored the first goal in Union history also scored the most goals in Union history. That player was Sebastien Le Toux.

Le Toux is considered the finest player to ever wear the Philadelphia uniform. The midfielder from France tallied first in that win over D.C. United on April 10, 2010. Then he just kept on scoring. He finished his Philadelphia career with 50 goals and 50 **assists**. They are both franchise records.

The Union has never boasted a League leader in any major category. But Le Toux was among the best in several seasons. He finished fourth among MLS players in goals and assists in 2010. He placed ninth in goals and fifth in assists in 2011. He also won Player of the Month honors in September that year. Le Toux tallied the second-most assists in the League in 2013.

Cristian Maidana (*right*) fights for the ball against Toronto FC's Jackson during a game in October 2015.

Another offensive standout for the Union was Cristian Maidana of Argentina. He joined the team in 2014 and finished that year eighth in Major League Soccer in assists. Maidana placed second in that same category in 2015. It marked the second time in three years that a Union player ranked second in assists in one season.

Jack McInerney (*left*) shoots past Toronto FC's Nathan Sturgis during a match in October 2011.

Perhaps the best short period of play in Union history was achieved by American forward Jack McInerney in 2013. McInerney was named MLS Player of the Month in both April and May that season. He finished seventh in the league with 12 goals.

The Union boasted two of the top scorers in Major League Soccer in 2017. That is when American forward C. J. Sapong placed eighth in the League with 16 goals. Midfielder Haris Medunjanin finished ninth in MLS the same year with 12 assists.

Philadelphia has boasted some fine goalkeepers as well. The best of the bunch was American Zac MacMath. He won 34 matches in his four years with the team. MacMath finished ninth in MLS in 2012 with a goals-against average (GAA) of 1.34 per game. He placed ninth again the following season with a GAA of 1.29. MacMath also holds the franchise record with 28 career **shutouts**, including 12 in 2013.

MacMath was indeed stingy when it came to yielding goals. But not as stingy as Faryd Mondrago of Colombia in 2011. Mondrago ranked third in MLS that year with a 1.06 goals-against average.

Goalkeeper Zac MacMath blocks a shot in July 2012.

Chapter Four

Defender Raymon Gaddis (*left*) and Toronto FC defender Justin Morrow battle for possession of the ball in March 2019.

The Union has not only boasted excellent scorers and goalkeepers. American defender Raymon Gaddis joined the team in 2012 and was still playing for Philadelphia in 2019. He played more than 14,000 minutes for the Union. That is the most in franchise history.

Fun Facts

1 Three Union standouts earned Player of the Week honors over the course of five weeks in 2016. American midfielder Chris Pontius snagged the award in Week 14. Midfielder Roland Alberg of the Netherlands earned it two weeks later. And midfielder Ilsinho of Brazil won it in Week 18.

2 Pontius earned 2016 MLS Comeback Player of the Year honors. He joined the Union after injury-filled seasons with D.C. United. He matched a career high with 12 goals in leading Philadelphia to its first playoff berth in five years.

Chris Pontius (*right*) in action against L.A. Galaxy's, Baggio in May 2016.

Living and Communicating

Some come from Europe. Others from South America. Or from Africa. They come from all over the world to play Major League Soccer. The League has more international players than those born in the United States.

But the transition is not easy. Many players from other countries do not speak English. They have never performed in America. They know little or nothing about the cities they visit. They must **adapt** to a whole new world.

The number of foreign-born players in MLS keeps growing. Only about four of every 10 minutes on the field in 2017 was spent by a U.S.-born player. That was down considerably from 2013.

Many new foreign players have arrived every year. Most of them must travel thousands of miles from their homes. They live in what is to them a strange place. Daily life is much harder than booting a ball away from an opponent or kicking it into a net.

They must learn a new language. They miss their families back home. They are in a world of strangers. They try to make friends with people with whom they have nothing in common. They struggle to communicate with their new teammates and coaches. They must find a new place to live. They must learn how to buy things with bills and coins they had never seen.

Some foreign players bring their families with them to the U.S. But their loved ones face the same struggles in a new land. The adjustment period is even harder for those who have yet to learn English.

Chapter Five

The only comfort zone for such players should be the soccer field. But even that is difficult. They do not know their teammates. They must learn the strengths and weaknesses of new opponents. They do not understand what their teammates are saying on and off the field. They need help to recognize coaching commands. They cannot answer questions from the media without an **interpreter**.

Travel in the United States and Canada can feel strange and overwhelming. They are two of the largest countries in the world. Foreign-born players most often arrive from much smaller nations. They are used to traveling short distances to matches on buses or trains. They must get used to spending hours on planes and sleeping in hotels.

Time away from home is extensive. MLS teams often play on Saturday nights. But they leave on Thursday or Friday. Matches end late. Players do not return home until Sunday. Spending half their time on the road is usually easy for U.S. and Canadian players. It can be miserable for those who cannot speak English.

Every new city can be an adventure. Foreign players must even adjust to the weather. The weather is often the same throughout smaller countries. MLS players might have a Wednesday match in the scorching heat of Texas. Three days later they could play in rainy Portland. And the following week they might have to endure a freezing night in Canada.

Foreign players must adapt on the field to more than changing weather. Major League Soccer features a faster pace of play than is common in other parts of the world. Matches are won with talent. The best athletes thrive in MLS. There is less **strategy**. Foreign players often struggle until they get used to the speed of the game.

Adjusting to a new world and a new game takes time. But their talent and love for soccer shine through. Among the examples are players who have worn Philadelphia Union uniforms. Le Toux came from France. Medunjanin arrived from Bosnia. Mondrago is a native of Colombia.

Such standouts helped make MLS truly an international game. And they have helped the Union win many matches over the years.

Fun Facts

1. **The most successful head coach in Union history is Jim Curtin. He guided the team to more victories than previous coaches Piotr Nowak and John Hackworth combined. He also won a higher percentage of his matches.**

2. **Major League Soccer received a huge boost in 2007. That is when international superstar David Beckham joined the League by signing with the Los Angeles Galaxy. He led that team to two titles before retiring in 2013.**

What You **Should Know**

- Modern soccer began in England around 1830.
- Most places in the world call the game football except the United States, Canada, Japan, Korea, and Southeast Asia.
- For Philadelphia, the birthplace of America, modern soccer has attracted great fan attention.
- February 2018 marked 10th anniversary of the Philadelphia Union.
- The Union's first mascot was "hatched" out of a giant glowing egg at the Philadelphia Zoo. He is a snake named Phang.
- Player Sebastien Le Toux joined the Union in 2010. He had won Most Valuable Player honors in the United Soccer League in 2007.
- The largest home attendance in Union history remains its first home game with 34,870 fans on April 10, 2010.
- The Union had yet to win a playoff match through its first eight seasons.
- Le Toux scored the only playoff goal in eight years of Union soccer.
- Philadelphia hosted an MLS All-Star Game in 2012. The battle pitted the League's best against Premier League team Chelsea, which had dominated play in Europe.

Quick Stats

- 5 players played in all 34 games in a single season
- Sebastian Le Toux leads in career goals and assists with 50 each
- C.J. Sapong scored 16 goals in the 2017 season
- Zac MacMath holds record for goalkeeper wins, with 34 total

Philadelphia Timeline

2008 Major League Soccer awards Philadelphia a team as its 16th franchise.

2009 The Union nickname is established after a fan vote in January and February.

2010 The Union is shut out by the Seattle Sounders in their first-ever match.

2010 Sebastien Le Toux scores the first goal in Union history to help his team defeat D.C. United 3-2 for the first victory in team history. The attendance of 34,870 fans in Philadelphia remains a franchise record.

2011 The Union earns their first playoff spot but loses to Houston in an Eastern Conference semifinal match. Le Toux scores the first playoff goal ever for the Union.

2014 The Union struggles against Major League Soccer competition but places second in U.S. Open Cup play.

2015 The Union reaches their second straight U.S. Open Cup final.

2016 The Union earns a spot in the knockout round of the MLS playoffs, but fails to win a playoff match for the first time in franchise history.

2018 A third U.S. Open Cup spot in five years is earned by the Union.

Glossary

adapt
A change to make life better or easier

assist
A pass that leads directly to a goal scored

crest
An emblem or design

diversity
Different kinds of people

franchise
A sports organization that features a team

inaugural
The first ever

international
Anything to do with more than one country

interpreter
Person that allows people speaking two different languages to understand each other

MLS Cup
The championship match in Major League Soccer

ownership
To have or hold as property

playoffs
Series of sports games or matches held after the regular season to determine a champion

rival/rivalries
Higher level of competitive fire between teams

semifinals
Series of games or matches to determine which finalists will compete for championship

shutout
Holding an opponent without a goal

strategy
A careful plan or method

Further Reading

Gitlin, Marty. *Neymar: Soccer Superstar*. Chicago, Illinois: Britannica Educational Publishing, 2018.

Latham, Andrew. *Soccer Smarts for Kids: 60 Skills, Strategies, and Secrets.* Rockridge Press, 2016.

Roth, B.A. *David Beckham: Born to Play.* New York, New York: Grosset and Dunlap, 2007.

On the Internet

MLS Next

https://www.mlssoccer.com/next
This website details the future of Major League Soccer.

Philadelphia Union

https://www.philadelphiaunion.com/
This official Union site features photos, team news, videos, and statistics

Sebastian Le Toux profile

https://www.mlssoccer.com/players/sebastien-le-toux
Learn all about the greatest player in Union history on this site

Index

About the Author

About half of the 140 educational books written by Marty Gitlin are about sports. Included are many about soccer teams and stars. He has authored several books about Major League Soccer and is especially interested in the Philadelphia Union. Gitlin won more than 45 awards as a newspaper sportswriter before starting his book-writing career. Included among the honors was a first place for general excellence from the Associated Press.